# Puffin Books

## BLESSU AND DUMPLING

Meet the dumpy dachshund who longs to be long, and the baby elephant who longs to grow into his trunk.

In the first story, a baby elephant is suffering very badly from hay fever and although he's only small, he has a very large sneeze. 'BLESS YOU,' chorus all the elephants whenever he sneezes. Blessu grows slowly – except, that is, for his trunk – and his sneezing doesn't help one bit!

The second story is about Dumpling, who wishes she could grow as long and sausage-shaped as other dachshunds. When a witch's cat grants her wish, she becomes the longest dog ever.

Dick King-Smith was born near Bristol. After serving in the Grenadier Guards during the Second World War, he spent twenty years as a farmer in Gloucestershire, an experience which inspired many of his stories. He went on to teach at a village primary school. He had his first book published in 1978 and since then has written a great number of books, including *The Sheep-Pig* (winner of the *Guardian* Award), *The Mouse Butcher*, *The Fox Busters*, *Saddlebottom*, *George Speaks* and *Paddy's Pot of Gold*. He has also written four non-fiction books for Puffin: *Pets for Keeps*, *Country Watch*, *Town Watch* and *Water Watch*. He lives in Avon with his wife and has three children and ten grandchildren.

D0962854

# DICK KING-SMITH

# BLESSU
# AND DUMPLING

*Illustrated by Adriano Gon*

Puffin Books

PUFFIN BOOKS

Published by the Penguin Group
Penguin Books Ltd, 27 Wrights Lane, London W8 5TZ, England
Penguin Books USA Inc., 375 Hudson Street, New York, New York 10014, USA
Penguin Books Australia Ltd, Ringwood, Victoria, Australia
Penguin Books Canada Ltd, 10 Alcorn Avenue, Toronto, Ontario, Canada M4V 3B2
Penguin Books (NZ) Ltd, 182–190 Wairau Road, Auckland 10, New Zealand

Penguin Books Ltd, Registered Offices: Harmondsworth, Middlesex, England

First published separately by Hamish Hamilton 1986, 1990
Published in one volume, with new illustrations, as *Blessu and Dumpling* in
Puffin Books 1992
7 9 10 8 6

Text copyright © Fox Busters Ltd, 1992
Illustrations copyright © Adriano Gon, 1992
All rights reserved

Printed in England by Clays Ltd, St Ives plc
Filmset in Palatino

# CONTENTS

# BLESSU

Blessu was a very small elephant when he
sneezed for the first time.

The herd was moving slowly through
the tall elephant-grass, so tall that it hid
the legs of his mother and his aunties,

9

and reached halfway up the bodies of his bigger brothers and sisters.

But you couldn't see Blessu at all.

Down below, where he was walking,

the air was thick with pollen from the flowering elephant-grasses, and suddenly Blessu felt a strange tickly feeling at the base of his very small trunk.

Shutting his eyes and closing his mouth, he stuck his very small trunk straight out before him, and sneezed:

'AAARCHOOO!'

12

It wasn't the biggest sneeze in the world, but it was very big for a very small elephant.

'BLESS YOU!'

cried his mother and his aunties and his bigger brothers and sisters.

For a moment Blessu looked rather cowed. He did not know what they meant, and he thought he might have done something naughty. He hung his head and his ears drooped.

But the herd moved on through the tall elephant-grass without taking any

further notice of him, so he soon forgot to be unhappy.

Before long Blessu gave another sneeze, and another, and another, and each time he sneezed, his mother and his aunties and his bigger brothers and sisters cried:

'BLESS YOU!'

They did not say this to any of the
other elephants, Blessu noticed (because
none of the other elephants sneezed), so
he thought. 'That must be my name.'

At last the herd came out of the tall elephant-grass and went down to the river, to drink and to bathe, and Blessu stopped sneezing.

'Poor baby!' said his mother, touching the top of his hairy little head gently with the tip of her trunk. 'You've got awful hay fever.'

'And what a sneeze he's got!' said one
of his aunties. 'It's not the biggest sneeze
in the world, but it's very big for a very
small elephant.'

The months passed, and Blessu grew, very slowly, as elephants do. But so did his hay fever. Worse and worse it got and more and more he sneezed as the herd moved through the tall elephant-grass.

Every few minutes Blessu would shut his eyes and close his mouth and stick his very small trunk straight out before him and sneeze:

'AAAARCHOOOO!!'

And each time he sneezed, his mother and his aunties and his bigger brothers and sisters cried:

'BLESS YOU!'

But though Blessu was not growing very fast, one bit of him was.

It was his trunk. All that sneezing was stretching it.

Soon he had to carry it tightly curled up, so as not to trip on it.

'Poor baby!' said his mother. 'At this rate your trunk will soon be as long as mine.'

But Blessu only answered:

'AAAARCHOOOO!!'

'Don't worry, my dear,' said one of his
aunties. 'The longer the better, I should
think. He'll be able to reach higher up
into the trees than any elephant ever has,

and he'll be able to go deeper into the river (using his trunk as a snorkel).'

'Ah well,' said Blessu's mother. 'Soon the elephant-grass will finish flowering, and the poor little chap will stop sneezing.'

And it did.

And he did.

The years passed, and each year brought the season of the flowering of the elephant-grasses, that shed their pollen and made Blessu sneeze.

And each sneeze stretched that trunk of his just a little bit further.

By the time he was five years old, he could reach as high into the trees, and go as deep into the river (using his trunk as a snorkel) as his mother and his aunties.

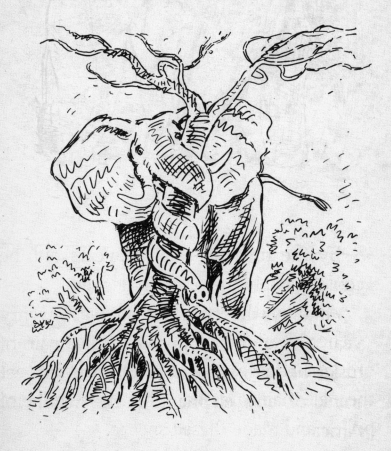

By the time he was ten years old, he could reach higher and go deeper.

And by the time Blessu was twenty year old, and had grown a fine pair of tusks, he had, without doubt, the longest trunk of any elephant in the whole of Africa.

And now, in the season of the flowering of the elephant-grasses, what a sneeze he had!

Shutting his eyes and closing his mouth, he stuck his amazingly long trunk straight out before him and sneezed:

'AAAAAARCHOOOOOOO!!!'

Woe betide anything that got in the way of that sneeze!

Young trees were uprooted, birds were blown whirling into the sky, small animals like antelope and gazelle were bowled over and over, larger creatures such as

zebra and wildebeest stampeded in panic before that mighty blast, and even the King of Beasts took care to be out of the line of fire of the biggest sneeze in the world.

So if ever you should be in Africa when the elephant-grass is in flower, and should chance to see a great tusker with the longest trunk you could possibly imagine – keep well away, and watch, and listen.

You will see that great tusker shut his eyes and close his mouth and stick his fantastically, unbelievably, impossibly long trunk straight out before him. And you will hear:

'AAAAAARCHOOOOOO!!!'

And then you know what to say, don't you?

'BLESSU!'

# DUMPLING

'Oh, how I long to be long!' said Dumpling.

'Who do you want to belong to?' asked one of her brothers.

'No, I don't mean *to belong*,' said Dumpling. 'I mean, to BE LONG!'

When the three dachshund puppies had been born, they had looked much like pups of any other breed.

Then, as they became older, the two brothers began to grow long, as dachshunds do. Their noses moved further and further away from their tail-tips.

But the third puppy stayed short and stumpy.

'How *long* you are getting,' said the lady who owned them all to the two brothers. She called one of them Joker because he was always playing silly games, and

the other one Thinker, because he liked
to sit and think deeply.

Then she looked at their sister and
shook her head.

'You are nice and healthy,' she said.
'Your eyes are bright and your coat is
shining and you're good and plump. But
dachshunds are supposed to have long
bodies, you know. And you haven't.
You're just a little dumpling.'

Dumpling asked her mother about the problem.

'Will I ever grow really long like Joker and Thinker?' she asked.

Her mother looked at her plump daughter and sighed.

'Time will tell,' she said.

Dumpling asked her brother, Joker.

'Joker,' she said. 'How can I grow longer?'

'That's easy, Dumpy,' said Joker. 'I'll hold your nose and Thinker will hold your tail and we'll stretch you.'

'Don't be silly, Joker,' said Thinker.

Thinker was a serious puppy. He did not like to play jokes. 'It would hurt Dumpy if we did that.'

'Well then, what shall I do, Thinker?' asked Dumpling.

Thinker thought deeply. Then he said, 'Try going for long walks. And it helps if you take very long steps.'

So Dumpling set off the next morning. All the dachshunds were out in the garden. The puppies' mother was snoozing in the sunshine.

Joker was playing a silly game pretending that a stick was a snake.

Thinker was sitting and thinking deeply.

Dumpling slipped away through a hole in the hedge.

Next to the garden was a wood, and she set off between the trees on her very short legs. She stepped out boldly, trying hard to imagine herself growing a tiny bit longer with each step.

Suddenly she bumped into a large black cat which was sitting under a yew tree.

'Oh, I beg your pardon!' said Dumpling.

'Granted,' said the cat. 'Where are you going?'

'Oh, nowhere special. I'm just taking a long walk. You see, I'm trying to grow longer,' and she went on to explain about dachshunds and how they should look.

'Everyone calls me Dumpling,' she said sadly. 'I wish I could be long.'

'Granted,' said the black cat again.

'What do you mean?' she said. 'Can you make me long?'

'Easy as winking,' said the cat, winking.

'I'm a witch's cat. I'll cast a spell on you. How long do you want to be?'

'Oh very, very long!' cried Dumpling excitedly. 'The longest dachshund ever!'

The black cat stared at her with his green eyes, and then he shut them and began to chant:

'Abra-cat-abra,
Hark to my song,
It will make you
Very long.'

The sound of the cat's voice died away and the wood was suddenly very still.

Then the cat gave himself a shake and opened his eyes.

'Remember,' he said, 'you asked for it.'

'Oh, thank you, thank you!' said Dumpling. 'I feel longer already. Will I see you again?'

'I shouldn't wonder,' said the cat.

Dumpling set off back towards the garden. The feeling of growing longer was lovely. She wagged her tail madly, and each wag seemed a little further away than the last.

She thought how surprised Joker and Thinker would be. She would be much longer than them.

'Dumpling, indeed!' she said. 'I will have to have a new name now, a very long one to match my new body.'

But then she began to find walking difficult. Her front feet knew where they were going, but her back feet acted very oddly. They seemed to be a long way behind her.

They kept tripping over things, and dropping into rabbit-holes.

They kept getting stuck among the bushes. She couldn't see her tail, so she went round a big tree to look for it and met it on the other side.

By now, she was wriggling on her tummy like a snake.

'Help!' yapped Dumpling at the top of her voice. 'Cat, come back, please!'

'Granted,' said the witch's cat, appearing suddenly beside her. 'What's the trouble now?'

'Oh please,' cried Dumpling, 'undo your spell!'

'Some people are never satisfied,' said the cat. Once more he stared at her with his green eyes.

Then he shut them and began to chant:

'Abra-cat-abra,
Hear my song,
It will make you
Short not long.'

Dumpling never forgot how wonderful it felt as her back feet came towards her front ones, and her tummy rose from the ground.

She hurried homewards, and squeezed her nice, comfortable, short, stumpy body through the hole in the hedge.

Joker and Thinker came galloping across the grass towards her.

How clumsy they look, she thought, with those silly long bodies.

'Where have you been, Dumpy?' shouted Joker.

'Did the exercise make you longer?' asked Thinker.

'No,' said Dumpling. 'But as a matter of fact, I'm quite happy as I am now.

'And that's about the long and the short of it!'